Tomi Ungerer

OTTO

The Autobiography of a Teddy Bear

I knew I was old when I found myself on display
in the window of an antique store.

I was made in Germany.

My earliest memories are of being stitched together in a workshop. It was quite painful! When my eyes were sewn on to my face, I had my first glimpse of a human being. A smiling lady held me and said, "Now look at this one, isn't he cute?"

Then I was wrapped up and snuggled in a box. It was very dark.

Soon I heard rustling and ripping noises, and the next
face I saw was that of a little boy cheering, and he hugged me.
His name was David, and I was his birthday present.

David's best friend, Oskar, lived next door.

They spent most of their time together, sharing jokes, stories and games. They called me Otto.

One day they decided to teach me how to write. With my clumsy paws I knocked over the ink pot, and splashed myself with purple ink. The indelible stain remained for the rest of my life.

Since handwriting was a failure, the boys fetched David's father's typewriter, which was much easier to use.

Life with David and Oskar was a lot of fun. We would play
all sorts of pranks. They would scare old Frau Schmidt
by dressing me as a ghost, lowering me on a piece of string
and swinging me across her window.

One day, Oskar asked his mother about the yellow star David had started to wear on his jacket.

"Mutti, look at David's star, can I have one like that?"
"I'm afraid you can't dear," she replied "because you are not a Jew."
"What is a Jew?" asked Oskar.
"Jews are different to us, they have another religion. The government is against them and makes life very difficult for them. It is unfair and very sad, but they must now wear this yellow star to be singled out."

Not long after, some men in black leather coats and others
in uniform came to take David and his parents away. As he was
leaving, David gave me to his best friend Oskar.

From the balcony I watched with Oskar as David and other people wearing yellow stars were loaded into a truck and driven away.

It was just the two of us. We missed David.
At bedtime we would talk about him and
remember all the good times we had together.

Another gloomy day was when we all went to the
railway station to say goodbye to Oskar's father. He had
become a soldier and was leaving for the front, where
the war was raging.

Then the bombings started.

When sirens wailed from the rooftops, we ran down to the cellar as quickly as possible to take shelter. Oskar always held me tight.

Whole streets were blown to pieces. Among the ruins and the fires lay innocent victims. Then one day a sudden explosion sent me flying in a cloud of smoke.

I was knocked out. I don't know how long I lay there. But it must have been several days before I woke up and found myself on a pile of charred rubble.

Everything was in ruins. Then came tanks and soldiers. There was a lot of shooting. I found myself in the middle of a raging battle.

Suddenly a soldier saw me and stopped.

He picked me up, and at that very moment I felt
a sudden piercing pain go right through my body.
The soldier, holding me to his chest, fell down
moaning. We had been hit by the same bullet.

Two men carried us away on a stretcher.
The wounded soldier, an American G.I., was
still clutching me against his bleeding chest.

His name was Charlie. We were taken to a hospital, where he kept me by his side. As he got better he mended the rip in my fur made by the bullet.

Charlie told all the nurses, "Look at him! Believe it or not this teddy bear saved my life. He took the brunt of the bullet meant to kill me."

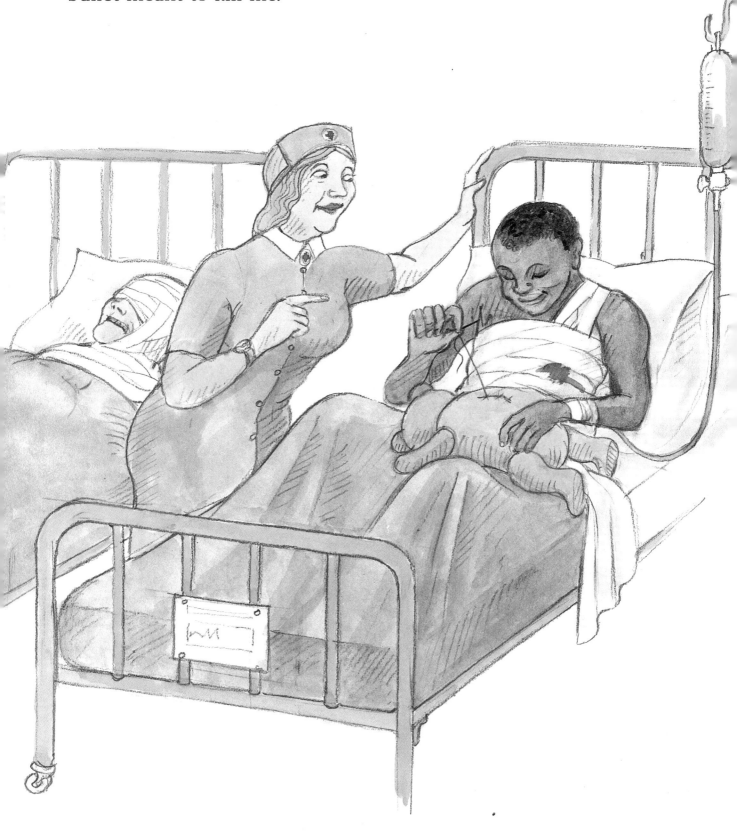

When G.I. Charlie received a medal for bravery, he pinned it to my chest. The story made the newspapers. My picture was shown all over the place. I was very proud of all the attention. Charlie renamed me Alamo, and I became the mascot of his regiment to bring the soldiers good luck.

When the war was over, Charlie went home to America and
took me with him. (By now I had learned enough English to
understand what was happening around me.) He pulled me
out of his army duffle bag and gave me to his little girl, Jasmin,
as a present. She was utterly delighted.

I had found a new home. Jasmin pampered me,
rocked me in her arms, and sang songs in my ears that
I had never heard before. I slept in a bed made out of
a cardboard box. It was bliss.

When Jasmin took me for a walk one day my happiness came to a brutal end. Three nasty boys snatched me away from her. They used me as a baseball and hit me with a bat. Jasmin called for help, but nobody came.

Half-blind, having lost an eye, battered,
ripped and caked with mud, I finally landed
in a trash can.

The next morning I was picked out of the trash by an old lady wearing a baggy sweater fastened with string. She put me in a rickety baby carriage full of rags and empty bottles.

She sold me to a man who had an antique store. He gave me a new eye, brushed off the mud, mended me and washed me.

"This is a very old bear. It's a collector's item," he said to himself, as he placed me in the store window.

There I sat, watching the world go by. No one wanted to buy me. Years and years passed, then, one rainy evening, a man stopped and stared at me through the window. He came into the shop and said with a heavy German accent, "That teddy bear in the window was mine when I was a child! I know it's him because of the purple mark on his face! How much does he cost?"

The man was my old friend Oskar! I was so pleased that he recognized me. He looked so different.

He took me home, and, for the second time, my picture appeared in the newspapers, this time beside the headline: "German War Survivor Finds Childhood Teddy Bear in American Antique Store."

In the same city a man read the story in the newspaper. Excited he immediately tracked Oskar down and telephoned him. When Oskar answered the call this is what I heard:

"Hello? Who? What? That's impossible! You're my friend David, and you live close by? Yes, Otto is here with me. We will come and see you right now. What's your address?"

We hurried into a taxi, and in an hour's time we were together again. David and Oskar talked and talked, and told each other what had happened since they had seen each other last.

David and his parents had been sent to a terrible prison. Both his parents died there. David had been very sick, but he managed to survive. Oskar's father had died at war, and Oskar and his mother were trapped in the ruins during the bombing. They were both wounded. His mother didn't manage to escape, but Oskar did.

Oskar and David had led lonely lives ever since, and now, reunited at last, they knew they would be much happier if they lived together. For the three of us life was finally what it should be: peacefully normal.

Since our happy reunion I have kept myself busy pounding out this story on my typewriter. Here it is.

Phaidon Press Limited
Regent's Wharf
All Saints Street
London, N1 9PA

Phaidon Press Inc.
180 Varick Street
New York, NY 10014

www.phaidon.com

This edition © 2010 Phaidon Press Limited
First published in German as *Otto*
Autobiographie eines Teddybären by Diogenes
© 1999 Diogenes Verlag AG Zürich

ISBN 978 0 7148 5766 4

A CIP catalogue record for this book is
available from the British Library.

Printed in China